Aussie Nibbles

The Littlest Pirate and the Stinky Ship

Nicholas Nosh and his pirate
crew are prisoners aboard Captain
Stinker's *Dirty Dog* – the smelliest,
most disgusting ship ever to set
sail. Can Nicholas find a way to
save them all?

Tick the
Aussie Nibbles
you have read!

☐ **THE LITTLEST PIRATE
AND THE STINKY SHIP**
Sherryl Clark
Illustrated by Tom Jellett

☐ **THE LITTLEST PIRATE
AND THE HAMMERHEADS**
Sherryl Clark
Illustrated by Tom Jellett

☐ **THE LITTLEST PIRATE
IN A PICKLE**
Sherryl Clark
Illustrated by Tom Jellett

☐ **THE LITTLEST PIRATE
AND THE TREASURE MAP**
Sherryl Clark
Illustrated by Tom Jellett

☐ **THE AMAZING FLEADINI**
Christina Miesen

☐ **SAM SULLIVAN'S SCOOTER**
Jane Godwin
Illustrated by Andrew Joyner

Visit us at puffin.com.au

Aussie Nibbles

The Littlest Pirate and the Stinky Ship

Sherryl Clark

Illustrated by Tom Jellett

Puffin Books

PUFFIN BOOKS

Published by the Penguin Group
Penguin Group (Australia)
707 Collins Street
Melbourne, Victoria 3008, Australia
(a division of Pearson Australia Group Pty Ltd)
Penguin Group (USA) Inc.
375 Hudson Street, New York, New York 10014, USA
Penguin Group (Canada)
90 Eglinton Avenue East, Suite 700,
Toronto ON M4P 2Y3, Canada
(a division of Pearson Penguin Canada Inc.)
Penguin Books Ltd
80 Strand, London WC2R 0RL, England
Penguin Ireland
25 St Stephen's Green, Dublin 2, Ireland
(a division of Penguin Books Ltd)
Penguin Books India Pvt Ltd
11, Community Centre, Panchsheel Park, New Delhi -110 017, India
Penguin Group (NZ)
67 Apollo Drive, Rosedale, Auckland 0632, New Zealand
(a division of Pearson New Zealand Ltd)
Penguin Books (South Africa) (Pty) Ltd
24 Sturdee Avenue, Rosebank, Johannesburg 2196, South Africa

Penguin Books Ltd, Registered Offices: 80 Strand, London WC2R 0RL, England

First published by Penguin Group (Australia), 2012

1 3 5 7 9 10 8 6 4 2

Text copyright © Sherryl Clark, 2013
Illustrations copyright © Tom Jellett, 2013

The moral right of the author and illustrator has been asserted.

Text and cover design by Karen Scott © Penguin Group (Australia)
Series designed by Cameron Midson, based on an original series design by Melissa Fraser
Typeset in New Century Schoolbook by Post Pre-press Group, Brisbane, Queensland
Printed and bound in Australia by McPherson's Printing Group, Maryborough, Victoria

National Library of Australia
Cataloguing-in-Publication data:

Clark, Sherryl.
The littlest pirate and the stinky ship / Sherryl Clark;
illustrated by Tom Jellett.
ISBN 978 0 14 330662 7 (pbk.)
Aussie nibbles.
Pirates – Juvenile fiction.
Jellett, Tom.

A823.3

puffin.com.au

For Mia and Dion. *S.C.*

For Joshua and Aiden. *T.J.*

Chapter 1

Nicholas Nosh, the littlest pirate in the world, was planning a huge party for his birthday. He'd sailed to faraway lands and now he was heading home in the *Golden Pudding*.

Gretta, his first mate

and cook, had been preparing
lots of party food. The
Pudding's hold was full of
cakes, pies and sausage rolls.

They'd been sailing for
two days and nights when,
before dawn on the third
day, everyone was woken

by a terrible smell.

'Eeuuwww,' said Gretta.
'Maybe some of our food
has gone rotten.'

4

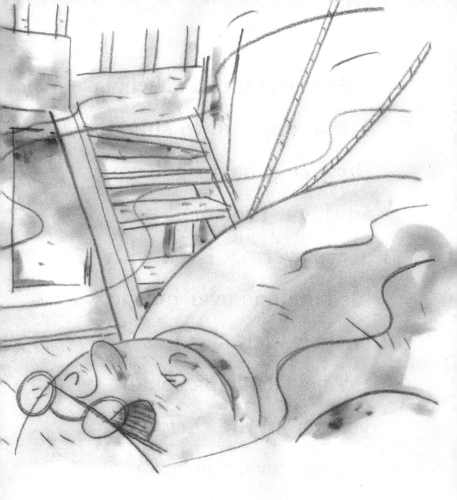

Nicholas went up on deck.
The smell was much worse
there, and the lookout
pirate had fainted.

As the sun rose, Nicholas saw a huge brown ship, the *Dirty Dog*, bearing down on them. The smell was overpowering. Even with his bandana over his face, Nicholas felt sick.

'Ahoy!' called a rough voice from the *Dirty Dog*. 'Surrender or be sunk!'

'Man the cannons!' Nicholas ordered.

Nobody moved. His crew were all lying on the deck,

looking green. Gretta sat
by the ship's wheel, holding
her tummy.

Within minutes the *Dirty
Dog* had come alongside

the *Golden Pudding*. A
large pirate jumped across,
followed by his men.

The big pirate's tummy
was so huge that he

needed three belts to keep
his pants up. He and his
pirates were covered in dirt.
Their hair was greasy, and
there were food dribbles on
their shirts.

'I'm Captain Stinker,' the
pirate said. 'And I want
your treasure. Hand it over.'

Chapter 2

When the pirates searched the *Golden Pudding*, all they found was party food.

Captain Stinker's eyes lit up. 'I'll take that,' he said. 'Men, store it in my cabin. And I'm short of crew,' he said to Nicholas, 'so I'll take

11

all of you, too.'

Nicholas and his crew were herded onto the *Dirty Dog*. The *Golden Pudding*

was left to drift away,
empty.

Nicholas felt terrible
that they'd been captured

without a fight. He counted
the *Dirty Dog*'s pirates.
'There are only six of them,'
he whispered to Gretta. 'We
could tackle them easily.'

'The stench is too bad,'
Gretta said. 'I feel so sick
I can't even pick up my
cutlass.'

Captain Stinker came

along the deck, followed
by dozens of blowflies. 'Get
working!' he shouted. He
pointed at Gretta. 'You can
be our new cook. Make me
some breakfast.'

Nicholas and his crew
staggered to their feet and
began trimming the sails.
Everyone had to sit down
and rest for a few minutes
when the smell became too
disgusting.

'How can you stand it?'

Nicholas asked Pong, one
of Stinker's pirates.

'It saves us needing to
fire our cannons,' Pong

replied. 'No one fights back, and Stinker gives us lots of treasure.'

'We're really sick of

porridge, though,' said Smelly, another pirate.

Nicholas was about to ask why when a large rat ran over his foot.

'Arrrggghh!' Nicholas could fight pirates of any size, but he hated rats.

'Shiver me timbers!' he growled. 'I'm really mad now. I'm not putting up with this!'

Chapter 3

The first thing Nicholas
had to do was get rid of
the rats. Down in the hold,
behind piles of treasure,
he found two large empty
barrels. He made holes in
the tops, and then he put in
lots of rotten food scraps.

Soon the barrels were
full of rats. They climbed
in through the holes and
couldn't get out.

When Nicholas went to the galley, Captain Stinker was there. He had sausage-roll crumbs in his beard.

'Cook, I want pancakes
for lunch,' Stinker said to
Gretta. 'Piles of them.'
'What about your crew?'

Gretta asked him.

'They can have porridge,'
Stinker said.

He stomped off.

'Stinker has been eating our party food,' Gretta said to Nicholas. 'He'll need another belt soon.'

She had scrubbed the stove, and the galley looked very tidy.

Nicholas looked around. 'What can we use to clean the rest of the ship?'

Gretta searched through the pantry. 'Here's a barrel of vinegar. That'll do.'

But when Nicholas took

the vinegar and some old
scrubbing brushes up to the
top deck, Captain Stinker
yelled, 'I don't want
a clean ship!'

'Why not?' Nicholas asked.

Captain Stinker leaned
down to Nicholas and
grinned. His mouth was
full of black teeth and his

breath stank like dead fish. Nicholas staggered backwards, trying not to throw up.

'My smelly ship is my secret weapon. Nobody can fight it,' Captain Stinker said. 'Get that vinegar out of my sight!'

Chapter 4

Nicholas went back to Gretta. 'We have to get Stinker out of the way so we can clean up,' he said.

Gretta held up a sack of prunes. 'I'll make pancakes with these. He'll be on the toilet for at least a day.'

Sure enough, her plan
worked. Stinker gobbled
down five plates of prune

pancakes. Soon loud groans
could be heard coming from
his cabin.

Nicholas and his crew set
to work. They fed all the
rotten food scraps to the
rats in the barrels. They

washed the ship with salt

water and then scrubbed

it with vinegar. With the

promise of a nice lunch,

Stinker's pirates helped,
too.

Gretta made everyone
toasted cheese sandwiches.

'Mmm, lovely,' Pong said.

'Why do you eat porridge
all the time?' Gretta asked.

'That's the only thing I
can cook,' Smelly said. 'Our
cook jumped ship. We were
hoping the captain would
share his food with us, but
he won't.'

Gretta made a big lemon

tart and everyone ate two
slices. Afterwards, Gretta
persuaded all Stinker's

pirates to have a bath, put
on clean shirts and trousers,
and brush their hair.

'I'd forgotten how nice a
clean shirt is,' Pong said.

When Stinker saw his

spotless ship, he was

furious. He ordered his men
to open the barrels of rats
and rotten food, and tip
them all over the deck.

'Your cook can make my dinner,' Stinker said to Nicholas. 'And after that I'm going to throw you all overboard. I want my ship back the way it was!'

Nicholas racked his brains. How could he save his crew?

Chapter 5

Gretta cooked ham and
eggs, and Stinker took a
huge plateful back to his
cabin. He'd made his pirates
put on their dirty clothes
again, and eat porridge
for their dinner. They sat
grumbling over their bowls.

'The party food must be
nearly all gone now,' Gretta
told them. That made them
grumble even more.

Nicholas had an idea. He
whispered it to Gretta, and
then they started talking
very loudly.

'I love your meat pies, Gretta,' Nicholas said. 'Lovely gravy and tasty meat with a splash of

tomato sauce. Mmm.'

Pong, Smelly and the
others started to drool.

'My favourite food is

apple sponge cake,' Gretta said. 'Crunchy apple slices, and sugar topping with fresh cream. Yum!'

One of Nicholas's crew joined in. 'No, the best thing of all is chocolate cake with cherries and nuts, and smooth, creamy icing.' He licked his lips. So did Stinker's pirates.

'What about Gretta's freshly baked bread with strawberry jam?'

said Nicholas. He rubbed
his tummy. 'Oh, I'll miss
that the most.'

'You can cook all those

wonderful things?' asked
Smelly.

'Of course,' said Gretta.
'But soon we're going

to be thrown overboard, so I'll never be able to cook scrumptious, delicious food ever again.'

'No,' said Nicholas. He sighed. 'You might have lots of treasure,' he said to Stinker's pirates, 'but you'll have to put up with porridge forever.'

The pirates looked at each other in horror.

Chapter 6

A plate came flying out of
Stinker's cabin. The crumbs
of a chocolate cake were
stuck to it. He'd been eating
more party food!

At the other end of the
ship, Stinker's pirates went
into a huddle. Nicholas and

Gretta waited, holding their
breath. In super-fast time,
the pirates came back.

'If you promise to cook all

those things for us,' Pong
said, 'we might change
sides.'

'Might?' Nicholas said.

Smelly smiled. 'There's
another condition. I want
Gretta to teach me how to
cook.'

'How about I invite you

all to my birthday party as
well?' Nicholas said.

It was a deal. The pirates'
mutiny took no time at all.
They put Captain Stinker

in a longboat and towed him behind the ship – a long way behind, because he was so smelly.

Stinker's pirates put on clean clothes again, and then everyone sat down to eat freshly baked apple cake. Pong presented Gretta with a lovely gold necklace as a thank you.

While Nicholas set a course for home, Gretta began to teach Smelly how

to cook. At first he burned
a few things, but he soon
got the hang of it.

The next day they found

the *Golden Pudding*.
Nicholas made Pong the
new captain of the *Dirty
Dog*, and Smelly baked

a cherry pie to celebrate.

When they reached port, Stinker's punishment was to have three baths in a row until he was clean. After that, he was given nothing but porridge to eat.

And he didn't get an invitation to Nicholas's birthday party, either!

From Sherryl Clark

I've always thought there might come a time when Nicholas and Gretta are captured! Who might be clever enough to do that? Well, nobody, unless they had a secret weapon. And then I thought about how a really bad smell can be so powerful that you can't do anything except maybe faint. Of course, someone who has that kind of secret weapon just has to be called Captain Stinker!

From Tom Jellett

I suppose we can't blame Captain Stinker for being a bit of a smellypants. I mean, if he's at sea for a long time, he can't have too many showers, or change his socks every day. I bet his ship would be even smellier if he fed his crew only baked beans, or if he left the milk out for a few days. I did this once, and that REALLY STINKS.

The Aussie Nibbles Story

In 1996, Puffin developed the Aussie Bites series as a response to the need for short chapter books to bridge the reading gap between picture books and novels. Our aim was to encourage confidence in young readers by providing them with well-written, relevant stories that were both easy to read and entertaining.

In 2000, due to popular demand, we expanded the series to include Aussie Nibbles, which are shorter stories aimed at younger readers who are tackling their very first chapter books.

The success of the Aussie Nibbles series has exceeded our wildest expectations. Nearly one million copies have been sold, and the books, which are produced entirely in Australia, are still in constant demand. Many of the titles have now been published internationally. Kids, parents and teachers love them, and they're easy to recognise by their trademark 'nibble' at the top of the book.

**Aussie Nibbles — helping children develop
a taste for reading!**